W9-DGX-250

07/2012

The School Bus Driver
from the
Black Lagoon

by Mike Thaler · pictures by Jared Lee

SCHOLASTIC INC.

New York Toronto London Auckland Sydney Mexico City New Delhi Hong Kong Buenos Aires

For Rebekah Faith, from Pa
—M.T.

To all the dedicated drivers who steer the big yellow buses
—J.L.

Library of Congress Catalog Card Number: 98-75201
ISBN-13: 978-0-439-06750-8
ISBN-10: 0-439-06750-2
Text copyright © 1999 by Mike Thaler.
Illustrations copyright © 1999 by Jared D. Lee Studio, Inc.
All rights reserved. Published by Scholastic Inc.
SCHOLASTIC and associated logos are trademarks
and/or registered trademarks of Scholastic Inc.

12 11 10 9 8 7 6 5 4   10 11 12 13 14/0

Printed in the U.S.A.
First printing, September 1999

40

We're getting a new bus driver this morning.
His name is T. Rex Fenderbender.
I wonder if the "T" stands for "Tyrannosaurus."

Eric heard that he's really a *cruel* bus driver and drives the *Magic Ghoul Bus*.

And Derek heard he lets his guide dog do most of the driving.

When you get on the bus, T. Rex tells you all the things he doesn't allow:

Then he tells you that your seat cushion can be used as a flotation unit in the unlikely event of a water landing.

The kids say that sometimes T. Rex
drives like he's in the Indy 500...

or the demolition derby...

when he's not practicing for
the Monster Truck Show.

Driving to school can be a *real* drag.
And when he puts on his helmet and shouts,
"Let's see what this baby can do!" you'll
wish you hadn't eaten breakfast.

I heard he collects stop signs and parking meters.

He thinks the school bus is an off-road vehicle, and that you're less likely to hit another car if you're on the sidewalk.

He not only *stops* at all railroad tracks—
he *drives* on them!
Getting there is *not* half the fun!

Freddie says that if there's a flat,
we have to change the tire.

If the engine breaks down, *we* have to fix it.

And he makes *us* pay for the gas out of our lunch money.

Randy says sometimes he gets lost— and won't ask for directions until you're in the boondocks.

Eventually, they say, you make it to school.

But he doesn't stop.
You have to jump out...while he's moving!

Uh-oh. There's the bus!
It's stopping for me.
The door's opening.

Hey, he doesn't look so bad.
I guess he left his dog at home today.
He smiles and lets me sit up front.
Then he closes the door, turns off the flasher,
pulls in the stop sign, and slowly drives away.

Boy, I wish he'd go faster—
I've never been in the Indy 500!